WRIGHT MIDDLE LIBRARY

EDGE BOOKS™

FULL THROTTLE

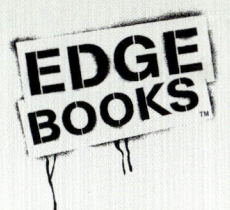

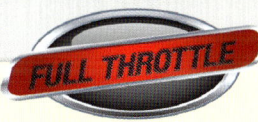

STOCK CARS

by
Melanie A. Howard

Consultant:
Suzanne Wise
Curator
Stock Car Racing Collection
Belk Library, Appalachian State University
Boone, North Carolina

CAPSTONE PRESS
a capstone imprint

Edge Books are published by Capstone Press,
151 Good Counsel Drive, P.O. Box 669, Mankato, Minnesota 56002.
www.capstonepub.com

Copyright © 2011 by Capstone Press, a Capstone imprint.
All rights reserved.
No part of this publication may be reproduced in whole or in part,
or stored in a retrieval system, or transmitted in any form or by any means,
electronic, mechanical, photocopying, recording, or otherwise, without
written permission of the publisher.
For information regarding permission, write to Capstone Press,
151 Good Counsel Drive, P.O. Box 669, Dept. R, Mankato, Minnesota 56002.

 Books published by Capstone Press are manufactured with paper containing at least 10 percent post-consumer waste.

Library of Congress Cataloging-in-Publication Data
Howard, Melanie A.
  Stock cars / by Melanie A. Howard.
    p. cm. — (Edge books. Full throttle)
  Includes bibliographical references and index.
  Summary: "Describes the history and design of NASCAR stock cars, as well as the races that they compete in"—Provided by publisher.
  ISBN 978-1-4296-4752-6 (library binding)
  1. Stock cars (Automobiles)—Juvenile literature. 2. Stock car racing—Juvenile literature. I. Title. II. Series.

TL236.28.H696 2011
796.72—dc22   2010000064

Editorial Credits
Carrie Braulick Sheely, editor; Ashlee Suker, designer; Laura Manthe,
    production specialist

Photo Credits
AP Images: John Russell, 27, The Morning News, Alison Sidlo, 4; Dreamstime: Actionsports/Walter Arce, cover, 6, 13, 18, 22, 24, 28, 29; Getty Images for NASCAR/Rusty Jarrett, 20; Getty Images Inc./Dozier Mobley, 17, Dozier Mobley/Don O'Reilly, 11, RacingOne, 8, 12, 15

Artistic Effects
Dreamstime: In-finity, Michaelkovachev; iStockphoto: Michael Irwin, Russell Tate; Shutterstock: Els Jooren, Fedorov Oleksiy, javarman, jgl247, Marilyn Volan, Pocike

The publisher does not endorse products whose logos may appear in images in this book.

Printed in the United States of America in Stevens Point, Wisconsin.
012011   006060R

Dueling Stock Cars	4
From Highways to Speedways	8
The Car of Tomorrow	18
Stock Cars on the Track	26
Glossary	30
Read More	31
Internet Sites	31
Index	32

1 DUELING STOCK CARS

Fans were on the edge of their seats as Kurt Busch's and Ricky Craven's cars ground against each other. The 2003 Carolina Dodge Dealers 400 race at Darlington Raceway was almost over. Only two laps remained as both drivers fought for the win. The slams even made Busch scrape the wall a few times.

The cars zoomed down the **frontstretch**. Nose to nose, they crossed the finish line. The finish was so close that it was hard to tell who had won. Luckily, the cars' computers were able to answer the question. Craven won by 0.002 seconds. It was the closest finish in NASCAR history.

Smoke trailed behind the cars of Craven (right) and Busch (left) as they "traded paint."

NOT YOUR AVERAGE CAR

Stock cars that race and everyday passenger cars look alike. The cars have similar shapes. The **model** names are even the same on the cars' noses.

But in reality, racing stock cars are very different from street cars. The "headlights" of a car in the NASCAR series aren't lights at all. They're just stickers! And don't expect to find a door handle on the car—there aren't any! Doors can fly open in a crash, leaving drivers unprotected. A driver enters and exits through the car's window.

model—a specific type of car, such as the Chevrolet Monte Carlo or the Dodge Avenger

frontstretch—the straight part of a racetrack where the race begins and ends

Fast Fact: NASCAR stands for the National Association for Stock Car Auto Racing. It organizes the most popular professional stock car races in the world.

Built for Speed

Other race cars, such as Indy cars, are actually more like stock cars than passenger cars are. Race cars are all built for speed. They use special tires for racing. Many race cars have **wings** to give drivers better control at high speeds.

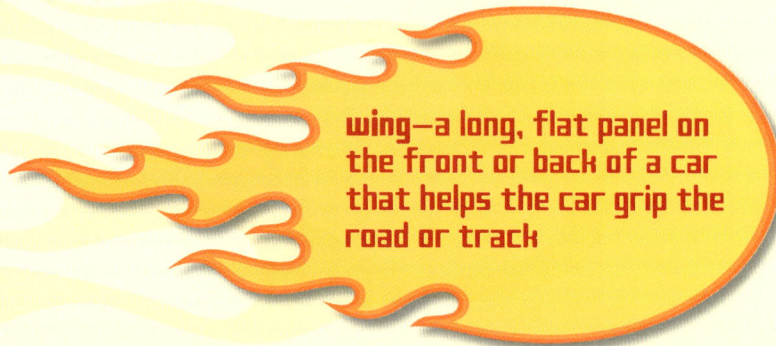

wing—a long, flat panel on the front or back of a car that helps the car grip the road or track

At Talladega Superspeedway, restrictor plates limit top speeds, which often forces the cars into tight packs.

Like other race cars, stock cars reach high speeds. In the past, stock cars have reached speeds of more than 200 miles (322 kilometers) per hour. Today, stock cars use **restrictor plates** on the fastest racetracks. These plates keep speeds near 180 miles (290 km) per hour. Driving faster has proven unsafe. NASCAR wants to protect its drivers. NASCAR also wants to make sure the cars are closely matched. That way, drivers have to depend more on their skill to win.

restrictor plate—a metal device that reduces a car's horsepower and speed by limiting airflow to the engine

Fast Fact: Sometimes stock cars use the same tracks as other race cars do. Both stock cars and Indy cars race at Indianapolis Motor Speedway.

2 FROM HIGHWAYS TO SPEEDWAYS

Drivers have been the superstars of NASCAR since the organization's beginning. Tim Flock, Glenn "Fireball" Roberts, Robert "Red" Byron, and other early drivers were fearless behind the wheel. More recent stars, including Dale Earnhardt Sr., Richard Petty, and Jeff Gordon, have shown the same competitive spirit. These drivers and their high-performance cars have drawn fans to NASCAR for more than 60 years.

Modifieds kicked up the sand of Daytona Beach in Florida at NASCAR's first race in 1948.

NASCAR TAKES OFF

People have been racing cars in the United States since the 1890s. Stock car racing became popular in the 1930s and 1940s, but the sport lacked standard rules. In the late 1940s, Bill France Sr. decided to organize stock car racing. France was a former race car driver who had become a race **promoter**. He wanted to set rules for stock car racing that would be the same at every track. In 1947, France met with 35 stock car drivers, race car owners, and track operators in Daytona Beach, Florida. With this meeting, NASCAR was born.

At first, NASCAR races featured older car models called Modifieds. Right after World War II (1939-1945) ended, new cars weren't very common. Factories had been making war supplies instead of cars.

promoter—a person or company that puts on a sporting event

Fast Fact: Modifieds were given their name because drivers made changes, or modifications, to their cars before racing them.

9

STRICTLY STOCK

In 1949, NASCAR's Strictly Stock races began. Strictly Stock races featured new models of cars available to the public. Early races were held at Daytona Beach in Florida and at Darlington Raceway in South Carolina. Other tracks were located in Michigan, Pennsylvania, New York, and Virginia. Most of these tracks had dirt surfaces. At Daytona Beach, the shore made up a section of the track.

Strictly Stock race cars were almost exactly like the cars everyone drove. Drivers made few updates besides painting a number on the doors. For safety reasons, they also taped down the headlights with masking tape. The cars were made of heavy steel. But the large, powerful V-8 engines had no trouble pushing the cars along. The cars reached top speeds near 100 miles (160 km) per hour.

Unfortunately, these cars had too few safety features. Tires blew often, causing drivers to lose control and crash. The doors were just strapped shut. In a crash, the doors could fly open, leaving drivers unprotected. Cars sometimes tipped or rolled after crashing. Rollovers could cause doors and roofs to cave in and hurt drivers. Some drivers were seriously injured or even killed in crashes.

Robert "Red" Byron speeds down the track in his Oldsmobile at Daytona Beach in 1950.

Fast Fact: Tim Flock put a trap door in the bottom of his race cars. He used it to check the wear of his right front tire.

11

Competing Companies

Stock car racing was dangerous. But this fact didn't stop manufacturers from trying to make faster cars. Ford, Chrysler, Chevrolet, and other manufacturers saw right away that having winning race cars led to more car sales. They quickly filled their catalogs with new high-performance parts. But they didn't do this just so the average person would buy them. High-performance parts in their catalogs meant racers could also use them.

In 1951, Hudson added Severe Usage Kits to its catalogs. The kits included a dual exhaust, a heavy-duty **suspension**, and high-performance engine parts. Hudson also introduced dual **carburetors** to its cars. All these additions made the Hudson Hornet the car to beat in the early 1950s.

Marshall Teague, along with other Hudson Hornet drivers, won 27 out of 34 NASCAR races in 1952.

The Daytona 500

The first Daytona 500 was held at Daytona Beach in 1959. The 40,000 fans gathered there to watch the race had high hopes. It was the first race on the new Daytona International Speedway. With a finish that was almost too close to call, the race didn't disappoint. Since then, fans have witnessed countless exciting Daytona 500 finishes.

Known as the "Super Bowl" of NASCAR, the Daytona 500 kicks off the racing season each February. The track is 2.5 miles (4 km) long. Its tri-oval shape looks similar to a triangle with rounded corners. Drivers race 200 laps around the track for a total of 500 miles (805 km). About 200,000 fans watch the Daytona 500 from the stands each year.

suspension—a system of springs and shock absorbers on a car

carburetor—a part that mixes oxygen with fuel before the mixture is forced into the engine's cylinders

AERO WARS

Hudson wasn't the only company trying to outdo competitors. Battles between Chrysler and Ford led both companies to make bigger, more powerful engines. Chrysler produced the monstrous 426-cubic-inch (6,981-cubic-centimeter) Hemi. Ford introduced the similar-sized Boss 427 and Boss 429. Both companies also began working on new **chassis** designs.

In the late 1960s, Chrysler and Ford rolled out their Aero cars. These cars had a sloped back that cut down on air resistance. The 1969 Chrysler Dodge Daytona was the most extreme. It had a sharply pointed nose and a high wing on the back to create more **downforce**. More downforce meant a tighter grip on the track.

chassis—the frame, wheels, and axles of a car, as well as the parts that hold its engine

downforce—the force of passing air pressing down on a moving vehicle

The Aero cars could go 200 miles (322 km) per hour. The high speeds were faster than the tires could handle. Drivers sometimes lost control when a tire blew, which caused crashes. Goodyear, the company that supplied the tires, tried to solve the problem. But the tires still shredded at speeds around 190 miles (306 km) per hour. Drivers continued getting injured in crashes. It was time to take action.

By 1970, the Aero cars from Dodge and Ford were sailing by the competition.

Fast Fact: The phrase "Win on Sunday, sell on Monday" came from the fierce competition between car manufacturers. It means that winning race cars spark a higher demand for their street-going versions.

NASCAR Cracks Down

In the summer of 1970, NASCAR required restrictor plates at all of its races. The lower speeds helped reduce the number of accidents. But the plates also reduced the advantage that Ford and Chrysler's bigger engines provided. For this reason, restrictor plates were a hotly argued change. Frustrated, Chrysler pulled out of NASCAR racing in 1971. By 1975, NASCAR had stopped using restrictor plates. Instead, NASCAR required smaller engines to keep speeds lower.

In the 1980s, manufacturers were making smaller, more fuel-efficient cars. NASCAR continued changing rules to keep competition safe and fair. **Spoilers** were added to keep the cars stable at high speeds. In 1987, Bill Elliott set the fastest speed in NASCAR history at Talladega Superspeedway in Alabama. He reached 212.809 miles (342.483 km) per hour. No driver has gone faster. That's because restrictor plates came back the next year after a bad crash at the same track.

spoiler—a winglike device attached to the back of a car; spoilers direct air downward for better grip of the rear tires

HITTING THE BIG TIME

Despite the lower speeds, NASCAR popularity boomed during the 1980s and 1990s. All the major TV networks wanted to be involved with NASCAR. At the tracks, promoters had to add more grandstands for all the people who wanted to watch. Drivers became household names. They appeared on cereal boxes and in sports magazines. It was clear that stock cars—along with their drivers—had hit the big time.

Jeff Gordon was one of the most popular drivers of the 1990s. He won his first championship title in 1995.

3 THE CAR OF TOMORROW

By 2000, NASCAR was more popular than ever. But in February, Dale Earnhardt Sr. was killed in a wreck at the Daytona 500. After this crash and others, NASCAR started work on the Car of Tomorrow (CoT). NASCAR wanted the car to be the safest, most competitive stock car ever made. At the same time, it wanted to reduce production costs. The CoT finally cruised onto the scene in March 2007. It is used in the Sprint Cup series, NASCAR's top racing level.

The Car of Tomorrow's front splitter helps the front end stay glued to the track.

THE CHASSIS

For the first time in NASCAR history, chassis became the same with the CoT's introduction. The CoT chassis has a wider, more boxy shape than stock cars before it. The body panels attached to the chassis are also made of stronger sheet metal.

Every car has a **front splitter**, roof strips, and roof flaps. Teams can adjust the front splitter to change the amount of downforce created. The strips keep the car from flipping if it turns sideways. The flaps keep the car from going up in the air if it gets turned sideways or backward.

front splitter—a panel on the bottom of a stock car's nose that catches air to create more downforce

Fast Fact: The original CoT design had a rear wing. But during the 2010 season, NASCAR began testing spoilers on the cars. Officials think spoilers might provide better handling than the rear wings do.

THE ENGINE

NASCAR stock cars don't have a standard engine. Instead, each company uses its own type of V-8 engine. For example, Toyota uses a Camry Racing V-8. Chevrolet uses an R07 V-8. NASCAR limits engine size. An engine can't be bigger than 358 cubic inches (5,867 cubic cm). Engines produce about 850 horsepower in the Sprint Cup series. The cars reach a top speed of about 180 miles (290 km) per hour.

Teams keep extra engines in the pits. They sometimes need to replace the engine during practice.

NASCAR engines and their street-model cousins work similarly. However, there are some differences. For example, NASCAR engines aren't fuel-injected. Instead, they have modified carburetors.

Carburetors vs. Fuel Injection

Street cars haven't used carburetors for about 30 years. Some NASCAR fans and teams think Sprint Cup engines should change to fuel injection. But others say that fuel injection adjustments by teams would be more difficult to oversee. They also say that fuel injection could lead to increased speeds and more crashes.

TIRES

Sprint Cup cars use tires called slicks. Goodyear provides about 18 different tire types for each race season. The type a crew uses depends on the track. Unlike street tires, slicks are smooth for better grip. They are also lighter than street tires to help the cars gain speed quickly. To maintain grip on the track, drivers make pit stops during races to replace the tires.

The Goodyear Lifeguard Inner Liner Safety Spare is tucked inside the tires. Similar to a spare tire, it allows the driver to get back to the pits if a tire goes flat.

Teams can go through as many as 12 sets of tires during a race.

Fast Fact: A tire for a street passenger car is built to go 50,000 miles (80,467 km) before wearing out. A racing slick only goes about 150 miles (241 km) before wearing out.

SPRINT CUP CARS AT A GLANCE

Chassis:	steel tubing
Body:	sheet metal at least 0.0247 inches (0.063 centimeters) thick
Height:	53.5 inches (135.89 centimeters)
Weight:	3,450 pounds (1,565 kilograms)
Length:	198.5 inches (504 centimeters)
Wheelbase: (distance between front and back tires)	110 inches (279 centimeters)
Engine type:	carbureted V-8
Engine size:	350 to 358 cubic inches (5,735 to 5,867 cubic centimeters)
Cost of engine:	at least $45,000
Top speed:	about 180 miles (290 kilometers) per hour with restrictor plates
Horsepower:	about 850
Transmission:	four-speed manual
Brakes:	four-wheel disc
Tires:	Goodyear racing slicks
Wheel weight:	24 pounds (10.9 kilograms)
Tread thickness:	1/8 inch (0.32 centimeter)
Cost per tire:	about $400

SAFETY

Safety is a top priority for NASCAR. The cars have several safety features you won't find on regular street cars. For example, stock cars have no glass. The windshield is made of shatterproof plastic called Lexan. A net covers the driver's window to keep the driver's head and arms from coming out.

NASCAR's CoT is loaded with safety features that its previous cars lacked. On the driver's side, foam padding is fitted underneath the body. The padding helps absorb the impact of a crash. Steel bars under the body on the driver's side also provide protection. The **roll cage** is larger and stronger than it once was. The gas tank, or fuel cell, is also stronger to reduce the risk of fire.

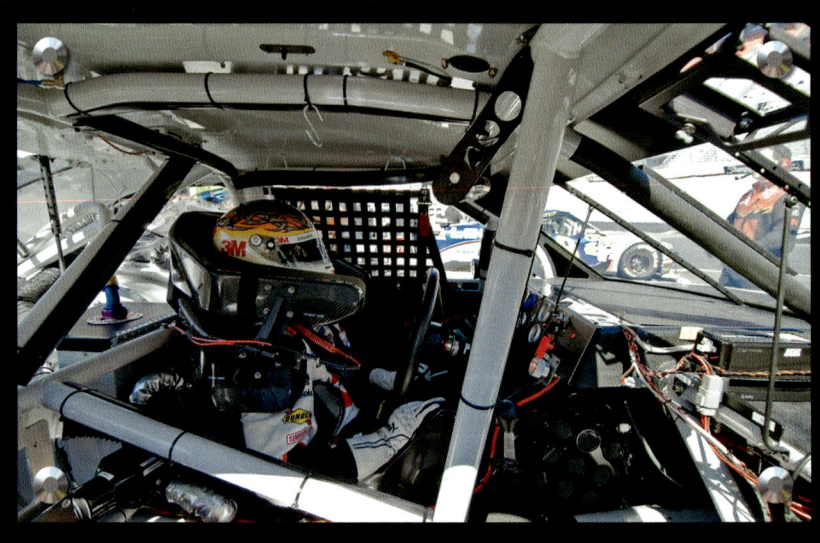

CoT designers moved the driver's seat toward the car's center to keep the driver safer in crashes.

IN THE DRIVER'S SEAT

Safety equipment isn't limited to the cars. Drivers wear safety gear from head to toe. The driver wears a fire-resistant suit, gloves, and shoes. A full-face helmet provides protection from head injuries. Since Dale Earnhardt Sr.'s fatal crash, drivers have worn the HANS (Head and Neck Support) device. This device helps keep the driver's head steady in a crash.

Stock car engines create a lot of heat. The inside of the car can reach 120 degrees Fahrenheit (49 degrees Celsius). The floorboards get so hot that drivers wear heat shields on the bottoms of their shoes. Cars also have a cooling system for drivers.

roll cage—a structure of strong metal tubing in a race car that surrounds and protects drivers

Fast Fact: *The rigid driver's seat hugs the body tightly to keep the driver from being thrown around.*

4 STOCK CARS ON THE TRACK

In 1993, several cars were jockeying for top positions in the Winston 500. Dale Earnhardt Sr. lost his lead. He charged forward to get it back. He tapped Rusty Wallace's car, causing Wallace to lose control.

Wallace's car flipped wildly down the track end over end. It came to a stop on the grassy infield. The car was torn to pieces. Its body panels were shredded and the roll cage showed through. Luckily, that same roll cage kept Wallace safe. He walked away from the accident with minor injuries.

Earnhardt's tap is an example of a popular race **strategy** called a "bump" gone wrong. Stock cars run into each other, sometimes by accident and sometimes on purpose. These bumps may cause the driver in front to spin out like Wallace did. But drivers' daring moves are all part of what makes stock car racing so exciting for fans.

strategy—a careful plan made to reach a goal

Kasey Kahne bumped Brent Sherman out of his way before winning the Food City 250 race in 2007.

Fast Fact: Dale Earnhardt Sr.'s very aggressive driving style earned him the nickname "the Intimidator."

27

STOCK CAR RACING BASICS

While there are other stock car racing series, the Sprint Cup Series is by far the most famous. Toyota, Ford, Chevrolet, and Dodge are the competing companies in NASCAR today. Each racing season starts in February and runs through November. There are currently 36 races each season. Up to 43 drivers can compete in a race.

NASCAR has three kinds of racetracks—short tracks, road courses, and superspeedways. Short tracks and superspeedways are oval tracks. Most superspeedways are at least 2 miles (3.2 km) long. Road courses have sharp twists and both left and right turns. All of the tracks are paved.

Before races, inspectors use metal frames called templates to be sure the cars meet design requirements.

NASCAR awards drivers points for their finishing positions in each race. After the 26th race, the 12 drivers with the most points compete in the Chase for the Sprint Cup. This 10-race battle determines which driver will become the season champion.

FULL SPEED AHEAD

Stock car racing has gained more fans than almost any other motorsport in the United States. More than 250 million people watch NASCAR races on TV each year. Five million more watch from the stands. With all this support, stock car racing is on the fast track to a bright future.

NASCAR's night races are highlights of the season for many fans.

Fast Fact: Racing organizations sometimes organize stock car races on local dirt tracks. The rules for these races vary from track to track.

29

GLOSSARY

carburetor (KAR-buh-ray-tur)—the part of an engine where air and fuel mix

chassis (CHA-see)—the frame, wheels, axles, and parts that hold the engine of a car

downforce (DOUN-fors)—the force of passing air pressing down on a moving vehicle

front splitter (FRUHNT SPLIT-ur)—a panel on the bottom of a stock car's nose that catches air to create more downforce

frontstretch (FRUHNT-strech)—the straight part of a racetrack where the race begins and ends

model (MOD-uhl)—a specific type of car, such as the Chevrolet Monte Carlo or the Dodge Avenger

promoter (pruh-MOH-tur)—a person or company that puts on a sporting event

restrictor plate (ri-STRIKT-ur PLAYT)—a device that limits the power of a race car's engine to slow the car

roll cage (ROHL KAYJ)—a structure of strong metal tubing in a stock car that surrounds and protects drivers

spoiler (SPOI-lur)—a winglike device attached to the back of a car that directs air downward for better rear-tire grip

strategy (STRAT-uh-jee)—a careful plan made to achieve a goal

suspension (suh-SPEN-shuhn)—a system of springs and shock absorbers that soften a car's up-and-down movements

wing (WING)—a long, flat panel attached to the back of a car that forces air downward to help the rear tires grip the track

Read More

Francis, Jim. *Stock Car Secrets*. NASCAR. New York: Crabtree Pub. Co., 2008.

Levy, Jancy. *Racing Through History: Stock Cars Then to Now*. Stock Car Racing. New York: Children's Press, 2007.

McCollum, Sean. *Racecars: The Ins and Outs of Stock Cars, Dragsters, and Open-Wheelers*. RPM. Mankato, Minn.: Capstone Press, 2010.

Roberts, Angela. *NASCAR's Greatest Drivers*. New York: Random House, 2009.

Internet Sites

FactHound offers a safe, fun way to find Internet sites related to this book. All of the sites on FactHound have been researched by our staff.

Here's all you do:

Visit *www.facthound.com*

FactHound will fetch the best sites for you!

Index

Aero cars, 14, 15

bumping, 26, 27

carburetors, 12, 21
Chase for the Sprint Cup, 29
chassis, 14, 19
crashes, 5, 10, 15, 16, 18, 21, 24, 25, 26

Daytona 500, 13, 18
Daytona Beach, 8, 9, 10, 11, 13
downforce, 14, 19
drivers
    Busch, Kurt, 4
    Byron, Robert, 8, 11
    Craven, Ricky, 4
    Earnhardt, Dale Sr., 8, 18, 25, 26, 27
    Elliott, Bill, 16
    Flock, Tim, 8, 11
    Gordon, Jeff, 8, 17
    Petty, Richard, 8
    Roberts, Glenn, 8
    Wallace, Rusty, 26

engines, 10, 12, 14, 16, 20, 21, 25

front splitter, 18, 19

HANS (Head and Neck Support) device, 25
Hudson Hornets, 12

Modifieds, 8, 9

point system (NASCAR), 29

racetracks, 7, 28
    Darlington Raceway, 4, 10
    Daytona International Speedway, 13
    Indianapolis Motor Speedway, 7
    Talladega Superspeedway, 6, 16
restrictor plates, 6, 7, 16
roll cages, 24, 26
roof flaps, 19
roof strips, 19

Severe Usage Kits, 12
slicks. *See* tires
spoilers, 16, 19
Strictly Stock races, 10

tires, 6, 10, 11, 15, 22

windshield, 24
wings, 6, 14, 19

WRIGHT MIDDLE LIBRARY